Twenty-First Centu[illegible]ste

An Anthology

'A space reserved for irony, sympathy and fond amusement'
Don DeLillo

Published in Great Britain 2013
By Brighton University Literary Society
brightonuls@gmail.com

Printed in Great Britain by Imprint Digital

Foreword: Literary Society

The Brighton University Literary Society presents to you poetry, short stories and flash fiction on the subject of

'Twenty-First Century Waste'

In his 1985 novel White Noise, which charts the wonder, debilitation and confusion of an ensuing age saturated by media and the homogeneity perpetuated by multinational corporations, Don DeLillo speaks of the need for a 'space reserved for irony, sympathy and fond amusement, the means by which we rescue ourselves from the past'. This anthology, we hope, is a 'space reserved for irony, sympathy and fond amusement', the work in it a 'means by which we rescue ourselves from the past'.

It is also a space for anger, mourning, loss, anxiety, despair – a renegotiation of the self in the modern age, a celebration of the endless cracks of sunlight that pierce the minutiae of contemporary experience. Our spit and sawdust contribution to this process is our bleary-eyed but enthusiastic attempt to compile a collection that engages in vital and complex ways with the modern world, which wonders aloud about the personal and political challenges of life in the early twenty-first century.

The volume of submissions was overwhelming, reading through them a humbling task. It only further cemented our belief that literature is a unique space – a place of relationship between text and reader wherein the friction of meaning occurs. We hope you enjoy the warmth of this friction.

Happy reading.

Brighton University Literary Society Editorial Team
Anila Arshad-Mehmood, Joel Roberts, Lauren Keen, Miriam Hemstock, Fiona Farquhar, Fred Stuart, Austin Macfadden, Eleanor Exton, Sophie Lloyd-Catchpole and Yasmin Jensen Giménez.

Six entries were shortlisted for Myriad Publishers (a Brighton-based independent publisher of original literary fiction and graphic novels) to choose the final winners, who were recipients of a cash prize. Martine McDonagh, author of *I Have Waited, and You Have Come* (2006) and *After Phoenix* (2013), chose them. They are:

1st - Does it breathe?
2nd - 21st Century Oil Painting
3rd - Sometimes

*

If you write, film, record, draw or create in any other way, we would love to showcase your work on our blog. Submissions can be made to brightonuls@gmail.com. No experience or previous publishing credits are required: the blog space is for you.

To get involved with the literary society or to put your work forward, please email:

brightonuls@gmail.com

To read other inspiring works of fiction:

Follow us on Twitter: twitter.com/whitenoisebtn
Or view our blog: facebook.com/whitenoisebrighton
Like our journal of undergraduate academic work on Facebook: facebook.com/brightonlinejournal

The Brighton University Literary Society would like to thank

Dr. Jess Moriarty

Kate Aughterson and the humanities department at the University of Brighton

Myriad Publishers

University of Brighton Students Union

The Springboard Grants Programme, without whose generous grant this publication would not be possible. For more information, please visit: brighton.ac.uk/alumni/funding-opportunities/springboard-grants-programme/

James Day-Cocking for taking the time to design the wonderful front and back cover

Finally, thanks to all those who contributed to the publication of this work.

University of Brighton

springboard
grants programme

Foreword: Jess Moriarty

In a time of escalating university fees, unemployment and the erosion of the welfare state and public sector, it is perhaps easy to understand why the theme of Twenty-First Century Waste resonated so strongly with students and staff studying and working in the universities of Brighton, Sussex, Chichester and the Open University. The idea of paying to further your education, all the while wondering if there will be a job out there for you when (if) you graduate and if, once you find that job, knowing that you will quite probably have to work into your late sixties or even seventies does not strike me as particularly motivating or uplifting. In higher education post-fees, the notion of the student who parties all day every day and hardly ever studies is a thing of folklore, mythology. Balancing academic work with a job and a social life, and working out who you are and what you might want to be is hard. It has always been hard but this seems to have been magnified and the tone and story-telling in the wonderful pieces of writing in this anthology are testament to that.

The antidote to all this anxiety, disillusionment and hopelessness is of course hope. Hope in the creative minds and exquisite writing of students and staff from the universities involved and hope in the form of the students in the School of Humanities at the University of Brighton who galvanised themselves into an editorial team, issued a call for writings that reflect the issues impacting on staff and students in higher education, edited and published this thought-provoking, beautiful and also devastating collection.

Huge thanks to the editorial board for working so hard to produce the anthology – incredible motivation and commitment. Thanks in particular to Anila Arshad-Mehmood and Joel Roberts who worked tirelessly and without any guidance or supervision to inspire their peers and develop this body of work from the initial idea to the collection you now hold in your hands.

As writers it is our job to commentate on the world, to offer a lens for the reader to look through and capture fragments of life – real and imagined. When you or I read this collection in the future, we will be able to look back and say 'yes, that is what it was like'.

Jess Moriarty

Hetty Cliss

Hetty is a third year English Literature student at the University of Brighton. Since finishing the Creative Writing module this year, Hetty has developed an appreciation for poetry, realising how difficult it is to write it well but how rewarding it can be when an idea comes together. Hetty has recently compiled a collection of intertextual poems, which has furthered her love of the form. Find out more at www.tumblr.com/acaseofknives.

Does it breathe?

I hear her ask, as I read over yet another line,

Yet another string of syllables:

Does it breathe?

I add another infernal metaphor, perhaps another internal rhyme,

Try to make the lines flow with the path of my mind,

Discover this no easy task, so read something of hers,

Something that breathes:

I read of crumbling lips, of letters addressed to a world

That cares not for reading;

I read more of her two-thousand scripts, my faith in my

Work ever receding;

I read of convulsion that is real and true, of sane madness,

Mad sanity, I read of her and want to be Nobody too and -

It breathes.

I read of desire for pleasure, then desire for death,
Each of these echo within me, I take another breath;

I read of Eden, of flies, of heaven, of grief,
Of ghosts, of death, of painting, of soul,
Of home, of summer, of fools, of belief,
And think there must be some hidden hole
In my work where life leaks out.
I sit at my desk, bite my pen,
She asks the question again
And - I breathe.

A Universally Acknowledged Truth

Am I nothing but a
universally acknowledged truth? The desire
to be combined, entwined, resigned to a
lifetime of companionship and unwashed
dishes? Forever surrounded by piles on piles of
clothes, stinking socks lingering between my
fingers as I pick them up for the third time this
week? Am I nothing but a socially
accepted ideal of beauty, vanity and maternity
forever expected to meet expectation,
never faltering from the norm? An
incandescent whirlwind of protection of
him, of me, of them? Am I nothing but
a trodden pebble on the path of destiny, a
path leading only to domestic bliss? I am not
a Goddess, by any means. Am I nothing
but who I should be?
Am I not me?

Liam Riley

Liam moved from Liverpool to London to work for a year in the newspaper industry before starting at Chichester University, where he is currently in the second year of his English and Creative Writing degree.

Sunday Night and Monday Morning

"It's light outside." Anthony replaced the curtain and, turning away, knocked the contents of an ashtray across the floor. "Christ. Do you still want to get a drink?" Anthony took a look at Owen's skin and felt his own cheeks.

"Nah lad. We'd end up just going to kip." Owen sorted through a pile of paper; throwing most to the floor but kept any marked 'DWP' on the arm of his chair. He lifted up a small bag, held it to the lamp next to him, and shook it. "We could go the shop anyway. Get some eggs." Anthony sat down and rubbed his palms together, laughing through his teeth.

"Again?" His eyes followed the bag as Owen placed it down.

"Well, it's something to do."

"Alright, just give me a minute." Anthony left the room and stumbled up the stairs. He opened the bathroom door and winced; vomit lining the toilet was curdling and beginning to form a skin. He flushed it away and tried to force his groin into submission. Giving up, he shuffled to the door and caught a glimpse of his disjointed reflection in the remnants of a mirror. He tried to confront himself but couldn't concentrate.

Anthony held on to the banister and descended the stairs meeting Owen in the hallway, leaning against the wall with his eyes half closed. After giving him a nudge they both left the house and walked close together down the street.

A rain cloud settled for the day, blocking the path of the sun, casting a muted shadow over the rows of red brick houses. The milkman's cart rattled from a distant corner and drizzle pattered on the tops of the bottles left behind. Anthony looked up to the roofs on the opposite side and saw a cat moving across the endless slate. Owen mumbled something to him but it didn't make any sense, he was distracted by the cat stopping and yawning. "We could go to Tom's?" He said, finally.

"Nah mate, he'll be working soon." Anthony narrowed his eyes as he saw the light emanating from the shop, "What a tool-"

"-A rusty fucking spanner." They both giggled nervously as they walked through the door. Owen ran his fingers through his hair. "What drink do you want?"

"I thought we were just getting eggs?"

"Shit, yeah." Owen went to the next aisle and picked up a pack of six eggs. He came back to Anthony and whispered, "Do you... do you mind going up the till?"

"You've got the money, haven't you?"

"Yeah but... fuck it, never mind." Owen went to the counter and Anthony waited by the door, picking through the newspaper stand. 'TOP BOSSES IN CITY FINED FOR MIS-SOLD VARIABLE RATE FUND'. He frowned and picked up another, 'LOCAL MAN STILL MISSING – Robert Douglas, 34, was last seen at the construction site, where he worked as the site's electrician, last Tuesday. Andrea Douglas, also 34, attended a press conference…' He looked at the accompanying picture, thinking he may be able to identify the man. He tried to focus on the image but put the paper down, choosing the *Daily Mirror* instead and turning it straight to the back page. He began making sense of the numbers but heard the till closing and Owen being asked if 'everything was okay?' Anthony noticed that his friend was already leaving the shop and followed him, as he turned his head back inside and called out. "Yeah mate, we're fine."

Outside, a car backfired and failed to start. They headed in the opposite direction from the noise, uphill. A man walking his dog appeared further down the road and without saying a word the pair crossed to the other side. "I can't stay long, got a meeting in the municipal building later," Owen said. The dog barked and the noise reverberated in all directions off the surrounding concrete, making them both flinch. Owen continued. "Got to work hard to keep someone else's roof over your head."

He picked up a milk bottle from outside a front door and they took a left, walking to the centre of a bridge that overlooked a disused railway line. Anthony took an egg out of the box and took aim at an empty, blackened signalman's hut. His shot missed. Owen put the milk bottle down and threw two eggs in quick succession, both of them narrowly missing. Anthony tried again and this time hit the wooden wall of the hut. They both watched silently as the yolk slowly spilt down the separate planks of wood, the stringy goo stretching to the floor, spreading into the dusty waste on the ground. Anthony forgot where he was. He stood there staring until the crash and splinter of the bottle Owen had thrown brought him back to his senses.

Owen laughed at his accomplishment and Anthony leaned against the wall of the bridge to look out at the view in the distance, of the north of the city. Owen stopped laughing and coughed instead. Recovering, he spoke to Anthony. "You know, when I was going to college on the train, I was obsessed with this place on the way there. We'd be coming up to a warehouse, one of the fastest parts of the journey, and we'd pass a big red sign. It was always at a sort of off-angle and two men in blue overalls, every time I looked, were trying to readjust it. Every time, they were there. I started to think, is there some meaning behind it? Maybe they were just carrying out regular maintenance, or maybe they were waiting for my train, every time? I've heard stranger things. Fuck, I've done stranger things!" Owen made a hacking sound in his throat and spat over the bridge, onto the tracks. "One time, the train had to slow down. I almost forgot. I looked up, with just enough time to see, and realised. They were just statues. Fucking statues. Pretending to fix a sign," he began to laugh again. "I can't even begin-" He looked for a response but Anthony wasn't smiling. Owen didn't have anything else to say, so he turned his head and looked were Anthony's eyes were set.

"Anyway, I've got to go." They both left the bridge from the way they came and, when approaching the shop, Owen remembered he'd left the rest of the eggs on the bridge. Further down the road Anthony spoke up.

"Owen. What does variable rate mean?"

Jela Webb

Jela Webb is a Senior Lecturer at the University of Brighton; her specialism is Information and Knowledge Management. She has authored articles, reports and is currently writing her second book in this subject area. In her spare time she attends live concerts and writes reviews for 'Maverick' magazine, 'No Depression' online magazine, as well as for Bob Harris' (BBC Radio 2) website.

Water..........in a word

Ablution. Aqua. Aquaplane. Aquarium. Aquatic. Aqueduct. Aqueous. Artesian. Bain-marie. Basin. Bath. Bathe. Bawl. Bay. Bayou. Beck. Bight. Boating. Bog. Boiling. Bore. Brine. Briny. Brook. Burn. Canal. Cascade. Channel. Cistern. Cloud. Cloudburst. Cold. Condensation. Conduit. Course. Cove. Creek. Cry. Culvert. Current. Dam. Damp. Dank. Deep. Deluge. Dew. Dilute. Diluvial. Dip. Ditch. Dive. Douse. Downpour. Drain. Drench. Dribble. Drink. Drip. Drizzle. Drop. Drown. Dunk. Dyke. Ebb. Eddy. Effluent. Estuary. Faucet. Fiord. Fishing. Fizzy. Float. Flood. Flow. Fluid. Flush. Fluvial. Flux. Fountain. Gargle. Geyser. Glug. Gulf. Gully. Gurgle. Gush. H2O. Hot. Humid. Hydrant. Immersion. Inlet. Irrigate. Irrigation. Jet. Lagoon. Lake. Leach. Leak. Levee. Liquid. Loch. Lock. Maelstrom. Marine. Mariner. Maritime. Marsh. Mere. Millpond. Mineral. Mist. Moat. Moist. Moisture. Monsoon. Nautical. Navy. Oasis. Ocean. Ooze. Overflow. Paddle. Pelt. Perspiration. Plunge. Pond. Pool. Pour. Precipitation. Puddle. Quagmire. Quench. Rapids. Reservoir. Rill. Rinse. River. Rivulet. Row. Runnel. Sailing. Saturate. Sea. Seashore. Seep. Shallow. Shower. Simmering. Sink. Sip. Siphon. Slake. Sleet. Slosh. Sluice. Slush. Snorkel. Soak. Sodden. Soggy. Soluble. Soused. Spa. Sparkling. Spatter. Spew. Spill. Splash. Splutter. Spout. Spray. Spring. Sprinkle. Sprinkler. Spurt. Squelch. Squirt. Steam. Steep. Still. Storm. Strait. Stream. Submerge. Suffuse. Surf. Surge. Swamp.

Sweat. Swim. Swirl. Tap. Tarn. Tears. Teem. Tepid. Thirst. Tide. Torrent. Trench. Tributary. Trickle. Tsunami. Umbrella. Vapor. Wade. Wash. Waterfall. Wave. Weep. Weir. Well. Wet. Whirlpool.

Matthew Mortlock
21
Brighton/Croydon, UK.
heteroglossia.

Om Blessed Nelumbo

To the whispering film of smoke, that along the river choke the very light from the air,

Lay underneath the plume, under the condensated looming, phosphorescent, drifting eerily – a small Nelumbo bud.

Upon the Ganges lay, and drifted, as if in the clouds uplifted, by the Priestess' song; spirited! In exultation to the Dead.

There still, behind the solemn craft, lay strewn (as if by hands, caste), a solemn train of purple Cupids, in juxtaposition of death.

Yet the umbre could not detract, from the thud; from the thunder of a thousand voices , as if through odd dialects a Gregorian chant airborne,

And so as if drifting in the notes, on intermittent light-shards float, smoke-bound, Pachamamma's petal ' d boats of defiance;

(though to the Dead, they make little difference).

Plaintively our flowers rest

Along the flaming shores of the embalmbed,

Purple then black, their beauty consumed,

Smouldering Heaven, a treaty, a treasure –

The Bless'd.

Untitled

How can a void, of nothing at all,

a tabula rasa, create?

Content, alone, a pencil drop

sends reverberations onto the slates;

blank, though receptive;

and the vibrations, echo

back words, no, not of truth

- but words of you.

Yugin Teo

Yugin Teo teaches film and literature at the University of Sussex and the University of Brighton. He has published poetry and short fiction with the Frogmore Press and in the Creative Writing Olympics Anthology (University of Brighton, 2010).

Broken In

A violation, possibly.
A revelation of sorts.
'How dare you look', says the exposed frame
of the vandalised coffee machine.

Containers, chemicals, pastel shades in sad plastic
connected via a person's whim and fancy –
the phenomenon of choice.
Funnelling into a strange gathering of sorts,
a confused concoction of
instant 2
instant 1
whitener/creamer
sugar
chocolate
all spawned by intestinal tubings of latex.

CASH FLOW® had been disrupted
by the wooden door wedge that had earlier gone missing.
Now resurfaced, broken at the tip,
party to a night's clandestine operation.

This once unbreakable drink machine met its match
though it still stands defiantly on the counter,
refusing to notice its burgled state,
its emptied cash box on the floor,
the ERROR message on the cracked display.

James Treadell

Currently a third year student/dinner lady at the University of Brighton and planning to study further - although which subject exactly he's unsure - he barely writes or has the time to, and will one day realise that he did have the time and should have been using it to do so. Possibly/possibly not a shame. He thinks perhaps philosophy.

Schisms

We are knowingly wasting more than what sustains us; we are wasting the ideas that are making the process so. – Anon.

I like to do things by my self.

A singular occurrence, as we all think, may be just that: singular. Singular in itself, momentary in happening and yet, when that one thing is realised in the minds of many, it becomes in reality something other than what it was. Such occurrences are then dealt with through this prism of understanding, and I don't like the idea of another person's decision being judged as that of my own.

I am powerless amidst the ensuing turn of events. Happenings understood myopically so that both unanimous and anonymous become the amnesiac mother and father of a refracted decision that no lone truth ever made.

Such a decision will, in time, come to form an idea.

So now, later, this idea grows and becomes the apparatus by which decisions are made. A thing in itself, that knows *something* and behaves in accordance to the knowledge from which it was borne. How long does it take for a certain knowledge to become aware of what exactly it is that it knows?

Soon it is there to witness one of those singular occurrences. Forever far from alone, it soon becomes apparent that this one happening has been witnessed by the provident scope of ideas: the past mimetic of present entropy.

Now it knows differently.

In later history, there is no way of saying for sure what, in the singular, actually happened. We also know that it was dealt with in just that fashion and that, prior to the happening, nobody could have known any differently. Do we know, now, knowing this, whether we ourselves know differently in accordance to the historic eventualities that we thought we knew differently from?

Who knows?

Jess Moriarty
With feedback from LA513 Semester 2

The Learner

Chewing gum grey bras hang off the radiator
while you and I lie in sheets of skin and
sweat. Too hot to touch, still to empty of
longing to want to. We meet at points that
were strangers just last night and now they share
the same dismal morning air. I thought that
student life would be about books and art,
men with unkempt facial hair and ideas
that promised to change the world from the safety
of the pub. I find myself choosing between super noodles
and solid, walking three miles to save money
for white wine that makes me retch on every
sip. I turn to see a face lost like mine;
needing answers to questions not found in
textbooks: Can I face another 2 hour
lecture? What am I doing here? Should I
call my mum and ask for just one more loan?

Sophie Lloyd-Catchpole

Second year English Literature Student at the University of Brighton.

Speak

I feel hot.

Red hot anger surges through me.

I press my lips together and I keep silent

as I've been taught.

When you're only seen and not heard, you learn

to hold your thoughts.

My mind whirs

and I beg my anger not to turn to tears.

I keep it, nurture it, I let it grow.

I lie awake

and hold rehearsals in my head,

words which should have been said.

It torments me,

so that when sleep comes I dream

in purple, white and green.

Maria Wallingford

Jug, Jug to Dirty Ears

We'd just met and she was leaving.

'Is it just the uni you don't like?' I asked with a cough.

Opposite, she squeezed her face between palms in a Munchy, screamy way. 'It's not about liking, is it. It's necessity.'

My head was pleasantly fuzzy. I poked around my plate, dividing leaves from roots, pushing it into places where it looked less troublesome. I chewed my lips, a dry and calorie-free habit.

They knew me in the cafés, which seems strange given I hardly ate. The intensity of these places pleased me. Around us coagulating fat was stirred into plastic bins. Blubbery men swabbed at stains on their ties.

Intensity, like I said.

This place was off campus. Our first meal. Our last meal. We'd met as those who knew counsellors and what it meant to be numb.

'So, what is it you're doing?' she asked.

'Being a student.' They did wine by the jug here and normally each jug made the wallpaper more jolly and easier to talk to. I studied her face and her plate.

'I mean, studying what?' she continued.

I shrugged and smiled. I hate to throw words away. 'Just... studying.'

She had a grey shininess around her eyes. She was leaving because the work made her ache in a way she'd failed to find enlightening. That, and it was all so damned unaffordable. When she stood up her dinner was there, mashed into the crevices of the chair.

'So, leaving to where?'

'Back home, don't know, maybe London. Somewhere to get money.'

The need to help was clammy on my skin. 'More money if you finish a degree, surely?' I argued, but she shook her head vigorously.

'Doesn't work that way. May as well bite the dust.'

'You mean the bullet.'

'Maybe.'

"Or the bottle. Vodka. That's what we need. You've not seen the best of this city. I know places that let you sit all day.' I knew the city too well of course, but in an unreal way. Still, I hated to know someone was giving up on it. 'You'll get through. If I did, anyone can.' She managed a bleak smile of her own and we talked about the work she'd been given.

I liked what she was doing; the fag butts of other

subjects were so fascinating. New stuff. Cool stuff.

What she needed of course was projects on the go and she was welcome to all of mine. Before we'd had the last dregs of another evening I'd planned we would do a book together, something where all the faraway tough-stuff of life could be squeezed into sentences that burrowed through riotous comedy pictures. She'd write, I'd draw - or maybe the other way round.

'Or...' – next time I was judiciously enthused by booze – 'We could blast it out digitally instead.' This was great. I planted these thoughts on a blog in case readers happened by. She seemed pleased. It made it all more real.

The future was suddenly magnificent and profuse.

Across the afternoons we warmed hands on coffee mugs and smoked enthusiastically, wafting each cigarette until it was three quarters gone, then mashing it and starting another.

Things like this consumed me, new things, promises. I'd made a habit of switching courses in the hope that not everything grew dull with time. When I was gifted a wary qualification I went postgrad through a knee-jerk fear of everything others were doing. Then I'd shifted topics, rewritten lots and scurried among a hailstorm of ideas, none of which were mine. Change was energising, wasn't it? A student, yes, forever warm and still to be enjoyed.

She began waking up to it, too. Over the days we thrilled at the flutter of creative prospects. In my room she looked at note books I'd begun, wild titling and promise, alongside digital devices full of odd words that one day I'd make into poems.

'You're wasted,' she murmured.

'I wish.' I saved my smile for the bottle neck, looking forward to the woozy infinity of a hangover when plans would re-muster their likelihood, along with those wonders we met through the screens' multi-liquorice lights.

Her own shared house had a grungy charm. There was a leak of rainwater and frecklings of mould clung mockingly to the walls. 'All part of the fun.' I told her.

'You're joking. Landlord should be strung up.'

I wouldn't have trusted any string this landlord might provide. The repair jobs that would have saved the place had never been done and now it was too late for anyone but low-lives or students.

'You get used to these things.' I said, optimistically. We lay on her damp carpet, half on top of the three bar electric fire, drinking.

'There's no more vodka. Shall we drink that?' I pointed

to a paper tray that held a dusty bottle of Montrachet.

No, that was given to her. She was saving it.

'Saving it for...?'

'Special occasion. Dunno. Leaving maybe. Or birthday.'

Instead we shared other things: wilder and better plans, a pack of cigarettes. 'You know, we need to do a social network project.'

'As well as the book?' She fidgeted, scratching at her forearms and wrists.

'Yes...or instead of, maybe.'

Among coughs and light-headedness, we planned our first e-book and our first publishing company. She must have been happy I'd found so much we could do together. For a moment she seemed halfway to staying.

With the morning brainscream, though, the plans ceased to bubble. As ideas became notions became fantasies and gradually melted back into our hangovers, I tried to eat a crust of toast and gagged miserably, eventually hugging myself to the toilet bowl and ignoring my housemates' shouts and bangs.

Quietly dazed, in a mirror in wintery daylight, we drew each other's faces and spoke of our sames and our differences.

'Why leave now?'

She sighed. 'Why do you love it so much?'

My finger bones pressed around sister vodka. 'You've got to stay for more of this,' I
said, hopefully – irritably perhaps. 'Finish your degree. Then...'

'Then I'm in debt and another year's gone by.'

'Well maybe we use that year.'

To inspire our seedling plans I showed her the pubs where the staff knew me and gave out extras and freebies. If we had enough of a laugh then surely it would help make her stay.

My own routines were simple but lovingly cherished. I got up at a respectable time for the pub, then wandered across campus for people to talk to, usually youngsters whose eyes crackled with thoughts.

What else would you want? And what else was there? An ailing father who I never saw but texted twice a month with a chirpy message, never mentioning food or work or completing or debt.

I just wanted a yes from her; a yes that she'd continue her course and learn how to live the life she'd found herself with.

In return she led me alongside her to the careers centre. I'd tried it before and got sick or scared or both. Did people still have careers? I was in touch with a few people who'd graduated with me. One or two of them worked behind the bar in the union.

'Maybe I could do waitressing,' she said with a resigned faintness. 'Pay my way a bit if I stayed. What about you?'

There was no point me getting a job. I needed the time too badly. Too many plans.

Instead, with a belief that vodka was best chilled, I suggested we drink on a park bench. Our new plans came with an attractive opalescence of breath. I had a musical animation aim now. 'It'll go viral, pow! Honest. Global popularity!'

'What about the book?'

Her lean features had regained their too frequent sadness.

'Book?'

'We were going to do the book together,' she said, with a glum disbelief. She was a ruminator.

'Yeah, but we can change it. This is better. Massive. What if...' I knew my plans had carried me somewhere she'd struggle to follow. For the first time I wondered whether she found my life admirable enough.

Pressing the neck of the bottle to her lips, I recorded our

whisper voices on my phone, something that would keep me in touch with that day.

In a rush of delusion we scoffed chocolate together and then took it in turns to hang ourselves over the toilet and nurse each other. My tongue was thick with vodka and the acid leavings of fat and process. The guilt was enormous and we nursed each other through that too.

She was still desperate to go. 'And what are you doing here anyway?' she spat.

'That's what my dad keeps asking.'

'Your dad?'

I explained he was ill, that I should visit but didn't. 'He says I need to stop this nonsense and get on with it.'

'With what? 'With life.' I felt my eyes prickle under fragile lids. 'But, I'd rather stay, stay and help.'

Her anger surfaced again briefly. 'It's not your business to help me.'

'No, it's just...' On the threadbare nylon carpet of her digs we tried once again for ideas that seemed bigger than the world and to wrap us up within them. Our tentative calories and carbs went one by one into the bin. Food was unnecessary. Cigarettes seemed enough.

Then the vodka ran out and we opened that lingering

bottle of Montrachet. It had been saved and saved towards a special enough occasion that had never come. It was booze. We drew the cork and swigged it.

'Stay.' I grew loud and was half crying. 'You have to.'

'Do I?'

'Yes. All our ideas. Your future. You're better than you know, better than...' My head floated in dubious independence and I ended up smashing the mirror with the bottle.

Everything was blurred, I fought towards that tight oval that had words for me, the mouth, the eyes, the world and all its everything. This was everything and food didn't matter. We laughed in our inflexible skins. I laughed my dizzy life as she did same-wise. Yes we laughed. I counted each second as though it were a pearl and hated the thought of parting.

That skin, a tight, taut, clingfilm around bones and a transparent parcel that is wrapped, ripped and crackling. Oh that skin. That little nonsense that had shrunk itself up and was something. Oh sanctuary that I loved.

The last day was especially cold. At a familiar café, I was sweeping at the i-pad, soberly reading through poems whose words I knew but had never understood.

'I've decided to stay,' she said. There was something

behind those words that was too tremendous ever to surface. There was a promise there that brought a new glow.

She had been to the doctor and was ready to feel her way back into life. The tutor had agreed to keep her on. Her studies had brought new understanding. She couldn't wait for more.

'So now?' she said with that crack-lipped smile.

I couldn't look up. 'So now, I've got to leave,' I mumbled. My head hurt. Everything hurt. This was leaving at its worst, and accepting it would take more time than I'd got left.

'No. Stay. Please.' I grinned. She wouldn't have understood if I'd thanked her. 'My father's ill,' I said, nonchalantly. 'I feel guilty for that and...and for all sorts of things. I'm going back home for starters.'

'Stay!' She blurted. 'Stay and we'll do that book. Why not?'

'You do it,' I replied. 'Make it work. Make it real'

She began to protest, perhaps wanting her own voice to collide with the world as it fell around her.

I knew, though, that life had already started elsewhere and that I needed to race to catch up with it, recognise it, persuade it back.

'A drink?'

She nodded, and as I rose from the chair my shoulders

felt the oncoming freedom of flight.

Sean Fleming

Sean Fleming. Aspiring writer, based in Brighton.
http://convolutednonsense.wordpress.com/

existential crisis no.43

here i am

3am

sleep is in the post

(sunday)

oh.

well, shit.

count sheep,

overthink.

huh.

isn't it funny how

the early hours foster

all manner of

perverted, profound &

ludicrous thoughts.

contemplating

oh messy

life.

or perhaps that's just me

(i doubt that)

William a. Watts

Splits his time between
Revelry at the pub and
skiing in Europe.

When burnt out days and faded nights,
Conspire to end in petty fights,
When jaded talk and wasted breath,
Leave one crying out for death,
When greying houses' façades crack,
And tumble in for want or lack,
When weary eyes survey the rubble,
Above cracked lips and dirty stubble,
When broken dreams and nagging fear,
Bridge day and night year upon year,
When open mouths gasp for a voice,
Or just the right to make a choice,
You will see the amassed hoard,
The young disenfranchised and bored.

Kieran Hughes

Male 22, moonlights as University Potwash; reads, writes, wrong.

My Occupation

IDF Basic Values – Human Dignity: 'The IDF and its soldiers are obligated to protect human dignity. Every human being is of value regardless of his or her origin, religion, nationality, gender, status or position.'

Why am I here?

I mean, I know *how* I'm here. I remember the letter, discussing our *options* in school, the glory of Zion and Eretz Israel. I remember the news reports, the car bombings and the dead children, the abyss of their wasted eyes... Or maybe the television didn't show us them.

'I can't fucking think in this heat. You want a drink?' Shiri jammed the butt of her rifle into the dehydrated earth but I didn't reply... I couldn't think either.

It's funny how you can know somebody for months and still only communicate through small talk. Although what could I say to her? That I'm having doubts? That I don't entirely believe in the validity of this occupation. That we don't meet with terrorists, we meet with ourselves. It would be stupid, she would just give me that look, that twitch of the eyelids that scorns and condemns, shamefully reserved for petulant animals and refuseniks.

I don't really fancy a year behind bars, but I feel like a charlatan. A refusenik refusing to refuse. Can I really be homogenised into one phrase, a phrase that barely makes sense? I guess that's quite fitting.

Why can't I just ignore it though? Why must I bear this unease? I read about those five *criminals,* the ones who refused to serve, sitting there awaiting their fate amidst comparisons to Mahatma Ghandi and Nelson Mandela. The whole thing seems quite unreal; as if it only exists to me, as if my memory is the only thing perpetuating their existence, maybe if I forgot about them I would be able to think like Shiri, think like my dad.

'What's wrong with you? You look fucking depressed.' Shiri glared at me, 'Our job is a calling, we are protecting our land! You should be happy.'

How did she know what I was thinking? Maybe she is right. If they would just disappear I wouldn't be standing here with a gun in my hand. I wouldn't have to wake up at five every morning to a cup of grey coffee and another day of heat and angst and boredom. It is their fault that I must guard this spot for hours, weeks, months. That I must sacrifice three years of my life. They are the germ of this lurching angst which stumbles drunkenly through my mind, making me question my education, the IDF, this holy war, the occupation...

I didn't notice the car until Shiri was stood in front of it, ushering the Arabs out. I can barely control my temper as I join her.

'I left my licence at home by mistake. I live here in Deir Ghassanah, so I can bring it to you in ten minutes.'

I start to tremble and can't look the man in the face, when I do it is completely featureless. It looks unreal. All I can do is yell with a plagiarised rage:

'THIS IS THE STATE OF ISRAEL, UNDERSTAND? YOU ARE DRIVING A CAR IN THE STATE OF ISRAEL.'

Ben Flowers

Accomplished writer, established poet and renaissance man:
Ben is none of these.
A firm believer that the mind is like the stomach: if you push it too hard all you get out of it is gas,
so spends most of his time trying to catch glimpses of inspiration in his peripheral vision.
http://toomuchmisinformation.blogspot.co.uk/

Today I am wearing wet pants.

Today I am wearing wet pants.
It's not a comfort thing;
it's not that I like the cold
dampness, or the slightly clingy feeling,
I just forgot to put them on the line,
that's all.

Today I am wearing wet pants.
It's not a medical thing;
it's not that I need them to
soothe a bruise like a wet flannel,
or to stop my thigh chaffing as I
walk around in wet pants,
nor is it to cool down some
burning haemorrhoids or to
fight some infection,
I just forgot to take them off
the line when it started to rain,
that's all.

Today I am wearing damp pants
(they've dried a bit since yesterday).
It's not a political thing;
I'm not trying to make some sort of

bold statement, or some radical
rejection of social norms in the form
of wet pants, nor am I trying to
stick it to the man for forcing
his taboo on wet pants, meaning
everyone associates wet pants
with having wet yourself,
when maybe it was just a cloudy day
and the dryer was broken,
that's all.

Today I am wearing no pants.
It's not a sexual thing,
I was just fed up of wearing wet pants.

Laura Hammond

Laura is a keen writer in her final year of Brighton University doing English Literature. After University she plans to get an internship in publishing, or do a diploma in secondary teaching in New Zealand. She will continue her writing and hope to get more published.

Wasted Souls

Those tears we cry

When darkness falls

Falls to no man's land

Where no man crawls.

Lie down now

Let the dreaming end

All will come again

Someday.

What once was

Wide eyed

Has passed to a different world

Waiting on the horizon

Is a new day

What is wasted

Is not always lost.

Waiting on the horizon

Wasted souls wait

Holding wasted breath

To touch again a cheek.

Not to fall to an endless night

But stand

Wide eyed again

In the new born light

To carry you home.

The waves will fall

Once a life

Reach for the surface

The horizon waits.

Rosie Smith

MAN IN A MESH VEST

COFFEE NUMBER TWO, WEAKER AND COLDER THAN THE FIRST. YOU ASK FOR A LIFE YOU CAN BELIEVE IN, YOU DREAM OF A LIFE YOU CANNOT LEAVE. YOU SMELL DEAD. YOU TASTE DEAD. YOU SAY "THIS IS A COUNTRY IN CRISIS. THIS A COUNTRY IN MORAL CRISIS," THEN YOU THROW UP ON YOUR SHOES. I WAKE UP FROM MY DREAM OF YOU AND I SMELL DEAD TOO. BREAK A SWEAT. BREAK A LEG. BREAK ANYTHING YOU CAN GET YOUR HANDS ON. THINGS ARE TELLING ME TO LOOK THE OTHER WAY, (MY RECENTLY CLOSED TABS WON'T OPEN. MY RECENTLY CLOSED TABS WON'T OPEN. YOU ARE AN ARTIST. YOU ARE AN ARTIST BUT YOU NEED TO TAKE A BATH. I'VE SEEN YOU AT YOUR WORST, I'VE SEEN YOU AT YOUR LOWEST EBB, AND IT'S BETTER THAN YOUR BEST. THESE WERE THE WORDS OF THE MAN IN THE MESH VEST.

Sometimes
you resist sleep and better judgement waiting for nothing short of an epiphany and all you get, as is the nature of any kind of TRYING, are the words EVERYTHING EVERYONE FUCK YOURSELF ALL THE TIME FOREVER FUCK YOU to drown out your non-existent problems.

Sometimes you just listen to John Maus and think about the time you choked on an ice cube while playing Buckaroo in the back of a car.

Sometimes you try and forget some horrible someone or something or sometime and all you get are ever-finer details of the situation until you have to go and eat cereal.

Sometimes you wonder if you could drown in the milk left over. Probably not.

Sometimes you wonder what your housemate could possibly have to shout about on Skype at three in the morning.

Sometimes you wonder if you should become one of those people who wears yellow shoes and paints fruit on the knees and elbows of all her clothing. I've never seen one of these people.

Sometimes you wonder if you should become a nun.

Sometimes you think about getting a bike.

Sometimes you think about getting a dog.

Sometimes you think about throwing up your dinner.

Sometimes you think about telling the truth.

Sometimes you don't.

James Burgess

James's taste in furniture leaves much to be desired. James is studying to be a paramedic. Life is an illusion in which he lives. There's nothing wrong with an illusion, as most of life such as love and hatred is a fabrication of your own mind. James projects these two emotions in his poetry at http://jim-bo-box.tumblr.com/.

Civics

Britain. The illusion sent from the sky,

A silhouette of hatred blinded by Her own demise,

We stole for years but 'civilised' the world,

Ever looked a little closer though and see what we unfold?

Mumbai children living on a landfill,

Wasted talent there was found and stolen by a film crew,

We'll do the right thing though and let the impecunious in,

Just pass the inane test before your citizenship begins, then

Stick them in a ghetto,

Tell them not to fear,

Everyone will look after you,

Even your killer we also allowed here,

Educate them poorly,

Drugs and violence gets them gold,

We created the hatred who

Carry the guns and knives we sold,

We push our new brothers to the devil,

Now our youth kills our youth,

All I hear is political subterfuge,

Just because you don't believe their god is the truth,

So now you shame the riots,

These 'monsters' have no respect,

But you gave them nothing to begin with,

So what really did you expect?

Fireworks, the almighty eye and smiles celebrated the new era,

We all stood side by side with excitement for our future,

Years down its clear to see we're in a state of collateral damage,

I dare you to stay ignorant and we'll see how well we manage,

Our end won't come from the editor - from terrorism or disease,

But the wasted votes on those, who claim to protect us and lead.

Bryony Lambert

Bryony is a fantastical dreamer living on the south coast. She is partial to glorious coffee, living beyond her means and lounging around looking fascinating.

"Write hard and clear about what hurts" You are not Ernest Hemingway

A deviant party trick, I once showed a boy how I can bend my arm backwards flat and aching towards my shoulder, an accomplishment if you can call it that. Flung forward from my wasted youth blossomed a repressed memory. I recollect an attempt to excavate my eyes, the known "windows to the soul" that have since found their pin-pricks abused, soft with misuse, grown to shut not absorb.

I have placed myself into an insidious prison; I daily confront the impassable mechanics of the human mind and whisper softly into pillows the lists I construe. It's often easier to think about my life in the form of bullet points rather than the fleeting moments I exist within which hold a stench of lost expectations.

I feel like a maddened Hamlet, the world has been lit ablaze by human disgust. The red-top news indulges its voyeuristic tendencies through anecdotes of other peoples misery, other peoples peripeteia. I feel saturated with tales I've heard mistakenly, they are the lives of strangers yet I often remember them as my own. Sometimes I think I belong in a landfill.

Squandered intelligentsia will not comfort you on your

deathbed; I've smothered myself with academic anticipation, perhaps genius cannot be bought with a student loan. Miserable like Havisham I live on my mattress, the television screeching, I hold conference to a polyamourous relationship with consumable media. I don't need to know how I feel, my chemical reactions are spoon fed into me. The throwaway lifestyle has left me on the precipice of panic, constantly swelling over. I forget how my lips look when they shape words, I'm not sure if I can scrape out barely a whisper in front of anyone.

Since fourteen I have fixated plasters on to the end of my fingers, I'm afraid of what human contact might scar me with. I remember climbing into my mother's bed during high school. I'd always have damp cheeks, which in turn made the bed sheets hold a curious vapor like sea salt. She would offer advice that I would gobble up, maternal wisdom which long lingered in the air after it had been spoken.

On the rare opportunities that you can see the stars in the urban sky I think I might have seen your left kneecap in the constellations. Now uncovered in the gloom, it seems more fragile than I can care to remember.

Most mornings I ache to remember my philosophy; "If I am not by default an intelligent girl with motives, enigma and aspirations then by default I am nothing at all".

Daniel Hibbs-Woodings

Daniel Hibbs-Woodings is a student from Manchester and studying at Brighton University. He strives to create pieces (be it in poetry or narrative) which reach out to an audience with a highly specific sociopolitical opinion, although any reader can feel privy to the emotions of that audience by means of a clear style and often highly simplified lexical choice.

Gold Flush

He scooped deep into the bowl,
upsetting the water so it splashed sloppily on the table as
he picked out the corpse of his newly deceased fish.
He let it sit in his hand for a moment, admiring the glaze
which had set so fast over its eyes like spare custard left to
cool.
A clear pool of liquid had begun seeping out of the fish
and was now gathering in his hand.
He rested his hand on the table (whilst keeping it cupped)
and watched the water drain out of the creature,
its body curled and its tail drooping pathetically over the side
of his hand.

How strange
he reflected as he stared at the fish,
strange.
He had always found the case of fairground fish marvellously
fascinating.
Capable of swimming in a sealed sandwich bag for millennia,
to the cuss of exhaust fumes and the wails of excited children,
but the moment they are won
(on a not so lucky game of hook-a-duck)
and taken back home,
they die
expectedly,

The moment they hit the water.

He sighed, tossed the fish in the bin,
and headed back to the fairground.
Maybe the next one wouldn't die.
Still, it was only a pound a try.

Jasmine Cowler

Third year English Language and Literature student with a passion for music, fashion & literature. www.thewildyouth.co.uk.

Harmonium

It is still day.
The last sunlight splinters through the ragged blackout and across the faded plush of the floor beneath, illuminating the cobwebs, the lines of light causing the dust to fall like rain.
Dreaming met its end here.
The song of the sparrows and starlings does not reach this place. They have sense enough to stay away, keeping to the skies and trees far, far away from here. All outside is still but for the caw of the crow, no one dares stray past the palace this close to nightfall for it is cursed as she is cursed. It does not do to linger near it too long. A lonesome straggler rushes past the twisted gate of thorns quickly and quietly, it is worth more than his and his family's lives to be caught here at nightfall.
The danger here is absolute.
She who resides here has survived the witch hunts of the centuries, she can be seen at night at the window of the highest tower piercing the black with her mournful eyes watching the distance as if to demand the highwaymen to abandon their pursuits and come to her, to comfort her, to be killed by her.
It was a luxurious place, once.
A broken harmonium stands in the farthest corner of the room, covered in spiders webs as if in its own imitation lace ball-gown, mirrors reach to the floor, their ornate metal frames now bronzed and rusted from time, an ancient dressing table lies littered with charms and exotic jewellery acquired from foreign lands and in the centre, perhaps the

most forbidding feature of all; an ebony coffin draped with purest black velvet. Ebony. The colour of Snow White's hair. The colour of tainted hearts. Inside lies the creature, she is of such sadness that your eyes would wither to lay eyes on her. Her beauty, such a comfort in life, is a curse in death. The constant reminder of why she is what she is. Her breath does not rise and fall like ours, the vermillion dress of satin she wears ,still, as she lies there in her half-death, her skin whiter than a mother witness to her stillborn, a transparency there betraying the navy veins that rest beneath her skin. Her sharp incisors, the obvious mark of her true nature rest upon her lips hard but there is no mortal blood to be drawn from them and at her neck so delicately shine a string of bright opals, the counter to her affliction, their power rendering her vampirity invisible, suppressible for just sixty empty minutes...

As the last shadows of day elongate and fade into black, her emerald eyes glitter through the darkness opening slowly and resignedly from the casket where she sleeps. She is tired. The kind of tiredness only known to those who are immortal and the tiredness consumes her like a drowning child is consumed by water. Her black hair cascades down her back like a waterfall as she languidly moves towards the window she has gazed out of for many solitary nights.

He had led her on the promise of something spectacular. She wonders if it will be tonight.

Joe Abercrombie

Joe Abercrombie is twenty-two, he studies English Literature at the University of Brighton. For more of his work visit joeabercrombie.tumblr.com

21st Century Oil Painting

Health and safety regulations,
terms and conditions apply,
license plates and registration,
omniscient electric eyes.

The crimson sand on the pavement,
the remnants of broken glass,
minimum wage enslavement,
a blazing abandoned car.

A married man's wondering hands,
the midnight street meat market,
subjective portraits of the damned,
the lumps of bile in vomit.

What bliss is there in ignorance,

the bitter sweet taste of decay,

there are no songs of innocence,

we that are bound, must obey.